世界の人々のこころをとらえた

３頭のくじら

THREE WHALES
WHO WON THE HEART OF THE WORLD

スザーン・キタ　文
スティーブ・サンドラム　絵
オーシロ笑美　訳
Written by Suzanne Kita
Illustrated by Steve Sundram
Japanese Translation by Emi Oshiro

COPYRIGHT©2000
ISLAND HERITAGE PUBLISHING
FIRST EDITION, THIRD PRINTING 2004

Address orders and correspondence to:
ISLAND HERITAGE
PUBLISHING
94-411 KŌʻAKI STREET,
WAIPAHU, HAWAIʻI 96797
ORDERS: (800) 468-2800
INFORMATION: (808) 564-8800
FAX: (808) 564-8877
www.islandheritage.com

世界の人々のこころをとらえた
３頭のくじら

THREE WHALES
WHO WON THE HEART OF THE WORLD

スザーン・キタ　文
スティーブ・サンドラム　絵
オーシロ笑美　訳

Written by Suzanne Kita
Illustrated by Steve Sundram
Japanese Translation by Emi Oshiro

ISLAND HERITAGE

　ラニはエメラルドグリーンの海にもぐり、口からあわをぶくぶく出しながらいきのつづくかぎりおよいだ。そしてぐっとみをかがめ、海底のすなを思いっきりけると、海面にむかってとびあがった。きらきらひかる波をつきぬけ、空中高くとびだしたと思うと、つぎのしゅんかん大きなしぶきを上げて海におち、ラニのからだで波をつくった。

　ラニはくじらになっていた。だって、ラニには大好きなくじらの友だちがいたんだもの。ラニがあんまりいつも海でおよいだりあそんだりしているものだから、ラニはまるで魚だね、とうちのみんながからかった。

2

Lani swam beneath the surface of the turquoise waters, blowing bubbles until she nearly ran out of breath. Then she crouched down, pressed her feet on the sandy bottom, and sprang toward the surface. She burst through the shimming surf high into the air, then fell with a great splash back into the ocean, creating her own waves.

She loved to pretend she was a whale. Why not? She had some special friends who were whales. And she loved to swim and play in the ocean so much that her family lovingly teased her about being part fish.

3

　ラニとザトウクジラの友だち、プトゥとシクとカニクにとって、今年のハワイの冬はさいこうだった。かわいいラニは海であそんでいるときいがいは、ずっと、この3頭のくじらがマウイ島のおきのあたたかい海で、ウエール・ウオッチングの人たちや、ちょうどそこにいあわせた人たちのために、とんだりはねたりのショーをしてみせるのをながめてすごした。

　このくじらたちが近くの海岸に来ると、なぜかラニにはわかるのだ。それに、かれらはときどきラニのためだけにショーをしているように見えた。くじらたちのすてきなショーに「マハロ！」と、大きなこえでありがとうを言って、こんどはラニがそのすばらしいげいとうをまねてみるのだった。

It had been a great Hawaiian winter for Lani and her whale friends, Putu, Siku and Kanik. When she wasn't busy playing in the water, lovely Lani spent her days watching the three humpback whales frolicking in the warm waters off Maui, practicing their water acrobatics for all the whale-watchers... and for anyone else who was lucky enough to be in the right place at the right time.

Lani somehow knew when they were near her shores, and sometimes it seemed that they would put on shows just for her. She shouted a fond "Mahalo!" to them to show her appreciation for their lively antics; then she would try to duplicate their fantastic feats.

CARTHIGINIAN

6

めすくじらのプトゥは海面をたたいてみせるのが大好きだった。からだをよこにたおして、３メートルもあるむなびれでパシッ、パシッ、パシッ、と水をたたくようすは、まるで自分で自分にはくしゅしているようだ。そうかと思うと、もっとはりきって、ごろんごろんとからだを右に左にかいてんさせながら、右ひれと左ひれでこうごに海面をたたいたりもした。ラニはこれを「プトゥの大かいてん打ち」とよんだ。

おすくじらのシクのとくいわざは、おびれで海面をたたくことだった。大きなしっぽを海の上高く持ち上げ、はば６メートルのおびれを海面に打ちおろす。バッシーン！まっ白なしぶきがふんすいのように上がり、すきとおったブルーの海におおぎがたに広がる。

もう１頭のおすくじら、石あたまのカニクが使うのは、そう、もちろん かれのあたま！水からあたまを出し、むなびれのところまでぐうっとそらしてから、ものすごいいきおいで海面にたたきつける。何かがばくはつしたような大きな水しぶきで、カニクがはるかなおきにいるときでもよく見えた。

ラニはプトゥとシクとカニクがとてもなかよしなのを知っていた。この３頭はぜったいけんかをしない。ラニはくじらがこいをするきせつには、なかよしの友だちどうしがてきになることもあると知っていたけれど、プトゥとシクとカニクはそんなふうにはならなかった。

Putu was especially fond of showing off her water slaps. She could roll over on one side and "slap, slap, slap" her ten-foot long flipper as if she were clapping her hands for herself. Or she could get really fancy and roll from side to side, slapping first one flipper, then the other. Lani called this her "super spinner" slap.

Siku's specialty was the fluke slap. He would raise his great tail high into the air and slap his 20-foot wide fluke down against the water — kersplash! — shooting white water out in a fan-shaped fountain across the crystal blue waters.

Hard-headed Kanik liked to slap with — you guessed it — his head! From out of the water, he'd near his head just up to his flipper-line, then he'd flop his head down with so much force that Lani could see the water explode even when he was far offshore.

Lani knew that Putu, Siku and Kanik were the best of friends. They never fought with each other. She also knew that during mating season, sometimes former friends became foes, but not Putu, Siku and Kanik.

ザトウクジラは「ポッド」とよばれる小さいむれをつくって、いっしょにたびをする。ひとつのポッドには1頭ずつお母さんくじらと赤ちゃんくじらがいる。それにたいてい、1頭いじょうのくじらが赤んぼうをそだてるお母さんくじらをまもるためにつきそっている。ふつう、むれのなかの何頭かはおすのくじらで、長いあいだいっしょにいるのもいるし、すぐいなくなるのもいる。ときどきこのおすたちは、自分がお母さんくじらと一ばんなかよくなりたいと思って、あらそうことがある。ラニは、くじらたちが友だちらしくないことをやりあっているのを見て、なんていけないんだ、と思ったことがある。

ある日、プトゥとシクとカニクと話していたラニは、どういうふうにけんかをするのか見たいので、うそのけんかをしてくれないかとたのんだ。くじらのトリオは、そういうえんぎをするのも おもしろいだろうと思ったので、ほんきでたたかうときのように、海にもぐってあわをふきだし、せんとうのじゅんびをした。

プトゥはペダンクルのパワーをじまんしようと思った。くじらのからだのしっぽがわの半分をペダンクルとよぶことはラニも知っている。ラニは小さいときからずっとくじらを見てきたので、くじらのからだのことなら、はなのもりあがったぶぶんからおびれのもようまで、ぜんぶ知っていた。ハワイ州の海洋ほにゅうどうぶつにきめられているザトウクジラはラニのおきにいりだった。

プトゥはよういのいちについた。おびれからじゅんに、からだを半分も海の上に持ち上げると、つぎのしゅんかん、それをかたがわの海にたたきつけた。それはほかのくじらを海の外へほうりだしてしまえるほどものすごいパワーだった！プトゥは友だちがだれも近くにいないことをたしかめてから、ラニにこの「プトゥのペダンクル」をしてみせたのだった。

ou see, humpback whales travel in small groups called "pods." Each pod has in it a mother whale, called a cow, and a baby whale, called a calf. And usually there are one or more other whales who act as friendly escorts and protect the mother who is nursing her calf. Usually among the escorts are a few males who stay for a short time or maybe for a long time. Sometimes these males will challenge each other because each one wants to be close to the cow. Lani had seen some whales demonstrate some not-so-friendly behaviors and, in her opinion, very bad manners toward each other.

One day while Lani was talking with her humpback friends, she asked Putu, Siku and Kanik if they'd pretend to be fighting, just so she could study their moves. The humpback trio agreed that this kind of performance would be fun, and blew some bubbles underwater to get ready for their fake fight, just as serious whale warriors do.

Putu wanted to show off her powerful peduncle slap. The peduncle is the back half of a whale, as Lani well understood. She knew all the parts of the whale from the nodules on their noses to the flakes on their flukes, for she had been a whale-watcher since she had been a small keiki. Humpback whales, honored as Hawaii's state marine mammal, were her favorites.

Putu got into position. Somehow she pushed herself up halfway out of the water, fluke first, then threw her whole tail to one side, creating a slap so forceful that it could actually lift another whale out of the water! She made sure that none of her friends was close by when she did her "Putu peduncle" for Lani.

カニクはいつものように自分がどんなに石あたまかをじまんしてやろうと思ったので、ずつきをしてみせることにした。これもきょうそうあいてのくじらをおどかすために使うわざだ。カニクはまず海面の下すれすれにおよいで、口を大きくあけ、のどに水をせいいっぱいためこんで、ものすごく大きくふくらませた。それから、とつぜん水しぶきをあげて海の上にとびだしたとき、もともと大きなからだが、ふくれあがったのどのせいでいっそうきょだいに見えた。ずつきのめいじんがほんとにけんかをするときは、とつぜんてきの目の前にとびだして、あいてをどっきりさせるのだ！

たかいがはげしくなると、くじらはたいあたりのこうげきをすることさえある。シクはこのこうげきを知っていたが、そんならんぼうなわざはラニには見せないほうがいいと思った。だいいち、だれかがけがをしてしまう！そのかわり、シクはすごいいきおいでしおをふき、しおは15メートルの高さまで上がった。ラニもこういうわざなら、大かんげいだった。

Kanik, once again eager to show off how hard-headed he was, decided to perform the head lunge, another move rival whales use to scare each other. First he skimmed the water just beneath its surface, then he opened his mouth wide and gulped down as much water as his throat would hold, causing it to bulge enormously. Suddenly he burst out of the water in a spray of ocean foam, looking even more gigantic than he really was because of his swollen throat. In a real fight, the head lunger would suddenly surface directly in front of the whale he wanted to frighten, with much success!

Siku knew that when the fighting really gets rough, a whale will even strike his competitor, throwing the weight of its own body against the other whale. Siku decided not to demonstrate this kind of blow to Lani. After all, somebody could get hurt! Instead, he blew a big blast from his air hole, one that shot spray 50 feet high into the air! Lani liked this kind of "blow" better, too.

ショーのフィナーレにくじらたちは3頭いっせいのジャンプ、「トリプル・ブリーチ」をしてみせた！3頭はまず、海の色がみどりがかった青からこいむらさきにかわるほどの深さまでもぐると、こんどはきゅうじょうしょうし、まるでロケットのようにどうじに海の上にとびだした。あんまり高くとんだので、くじらたちの大きなからだがほとんどぜんぶ見えた。「すごーい！」ラニがさけんだ。「カメラをもってくればよかった！でも、いいわ。きょうのショーはぜったいわすれないもの！」

To top off the show, the three whales presented Lani with a triple treat — a triple breach! They all sounded, diving deep down past the blue-green and into the dark purple water, then they burst upward like rockets through the ocean's surface all at the same time, jumping so high that almost all of their huge bodies could be seen. "Wow!" said Lani, "I wish I had a camera! But that's okay, I'll remember this show forever!"

　ラニはどうやってくじらを見わけているのだろう？ それはかんたんなんだ。くじらを
よく見ている人なら、だれでも知っているんだが、くじらのおびれには白と黒のも
ようがあって、それぞれみんなちがっている。人のしもんとおなじで、ぜったいに
おなじもようがない。プトゥとシクとカニクのおびれのもようもみんなちがっているのがわか
るかな？

　ラニはくじらたちがこんどは何をしているんだろう、もっと何か見せてくれるのかな
と思った。でも、そうじゃなかった。くじらたちはおびれを水の上にさしあげて、
さようならとふっているのだ。アラスカおきのつめたい海にもどるときが来たので、
これから長いたびに出る。かれらは毎年アラスカからハワイ、そして、ハワイからアラスカ
へと10、000キロもたびをする。

How did Lani know which whale was which? That's easy — any good whale-watcher knows that the fluke on each whale is covered with black and white markings that make it different from any other. The flukes are like the fingerprints on humans — no two are alike. See how Putu, Siku and Kanik have different markings on their flukes?

Lani wondered what these entertainers were up to now — more tricks? No, they were waving their flukes in the air to say good-bye, for it was time for them to start off on their long journey back to the cold northern waters off of Alaska. Every year they traveled about 6,000 miles from Alaska to Hawaii, then back again.

くじらたちがなぜ、こんなにきれいであたたかくて きもちのいいハワイをはなれて、つめたいほっきょくの海に行きたいのか、ラニにはわからなかった。「でも、行っちゃうんだ...。」ためいきをつくと、ラニはあいさつしているくじらたちにむかって、かなしそうに手をふった。「すばらしいショーをありがとう。アロハ。来年の冬、また会おうね。」友だちが行ってしまうとさびしくなる。

　カニクとシクとプトゥには、自分たちがどうして氷のようにつめたい北の海に行きたいのか、そして、行かなくちゃいけないのか、よくわかっていた。そこに行けば、小さい魚やプランクトンがおなかいっぱい食べられるのだ。朝ごはんも昼ごはんもおやつも晩ごはんも、みーんなすごいごちそうだぞ。かんがえただけでうれしくなったくじらたちは「みんなで波をつくろう！」とさけんだ。

　けれども、この年はかれらにとって、いつもとずいぶんちがう年になった。自分たちが世界てきにゆうめいなくじらになるなんて、だれにそうぞうできただろう。そして、つぎの冬、ラニに会いにかえるのは、2頭だけだということも。

She wondered why they would want to leave beautiful, warm, friendly Hawaii for the cold waters of the Arctic Ocean? "Oh, well, " she sighed, sadly waving her own good-bye as they waved theirs, "Thanks for the great show. Aloha, and I'll see you next winter." She would miss her friends.

Kanik, Siku and Putu knew very well why they wanted and needed to return to the frigid northern waters. They loved to feed on the abundant supply of small fish and plankton there. "Let's make waves!" the friends shouted enthusiastically, as they imagined the great breakfasts, lunches, snacks and dinners that awaited them.

But this year, things were going to be very different for Siku, Kanik and Putu. They didn't know it, but they were going to become world-famous whales. They also didn't know that only two of them would return to visit Lani next winter.

北にむかうたびは、けっこうゆかいでおもしろかったが、2か月いじょうもかかるものだった。3頭のくじらは道々うたをうたって、ときをすごした。くじらのうたはソロでもコーラスでも、とてもかわいい。かれらは海のうつくしさと、そこに住むすべての生き物のことをうたった。どっちのほうこうに行こうかと、かんがえなくてもよかった。なぜなら、ちきゅうには、「地磁気の道」とよばれる道がたてよこにはしっていて、それにそって行きさえすればよかったのだから。きせつてきにいどうする生き物は、みんなこうしてたびをする。

22

The trip up north was really quite fun and interesting, but it took them more than two months. To pass the time, the friends sang songs along the way. Whale music is quite lovely, whether sung in chorus or solo. They sang about the beauty of their underwater world and all of its creatures. And they hardly had to think about where they were going, since they just followed what some scientists now call the "magnetic roadways" that crisscross our globe. That's how many migrating creatures find their way.

シクとカニクとプトゥは、やっとほっきょくのわがやについた。アメリカでいちばん北のとち、アラスカのバローみさきのおきだ。かれらはハワイにいるとき、アメリカでいちばん南のちてん、サウスポイントにも行ったから、アメリカのはしからはしまで知っていることになる。

　長いたびだったけど、来てよかった。3頭はひといきつくと、すぐ友だちのデナリをさがした。デナリはユピクエスキモーの少年で、ハワイのラニと同じように「くじらと話す」ことができる。じつは、このくじらたちの名前は、ある夏デナリがはじめてかれらに会って、友だちになったときにつけたものだった。プトゥは「氷のあな」、シクは「氷」、カニクは「ひとひらの雪」といういみだ。さいしょの二つの名前はくじらたちにぴったりだけど、石あたまの雪って、いったいどういうんだろう？

Siku, Kanik and Putu finally got to the place they called their arctic home, the waters off the northernmost point in the United States — Point Barrow, Alaska. You could say that these whales knew the U.S. from top to bottom, since they had also visited South Point, the southernmost point in the United States, during their visit to Hawaii.

The long trip was well worth it. Right after they got settled in, they looked for their friend, Denali, a Yupik Eskimo boy who "talked whale" just like Lani did in Hawaii. In fact, Denali had been the one to name these whales when they met and became buddies that first summer. Putu is the word for "Ice Hole," Siku means "Ice" and Kanik was named "Snowflake." The first two names fit perfectly, but who ever heard of a hard-headed snowflake?

じらたちがさがすまでもなく、友だちが自分のあそびばにもどってきたのを見て、大よろこびのデナリがユピク語でうれしそうにあいさつをした。「カマイ！」くじらたちは長いりょこうのあとでおなかがぺこぺこだったから、「やあ、デナリ、またあとでね。」と言うと、大いそぎでごちそうを食べにいった。5,000キロもたびをしたのはこのためだもの。

They didn't waste much time catching up on things with Denali, who greeted them with a Yupik hello. "Camai!" he cried out joyfully, so happy to see them back in his own backyard. The world travelers were so hungry that after a quick "Hi, Denali! Catch you later!," the three pals hurried off to begin the tasty feast they'd traveled 3,000 miles to enjoy.

デナリは夏のよていをこなしていきながら、ときどきくじらたちをながめた。夏は日が長くてよかった。おかげで、もっとゆっくりくじらを見ることができる。デナリもラニとおなじように、このなかよしトリオがいつ、どこにあらわれるかわかるのだった。ときどき夜のおいのりをすませてからも、くじらになった自分をそうぞうしてねむれないときがあった。ざんねんなことに、ここの海の水はあんまりつめたすぎて、ラニのように海にもぐったりあそんだりすることはできなかった。

エスキモーの人たちはたいていみんな、たくさんのくじらのにくを食べる。デナリも食べた。けれども、もちろん、この３頭の友だちはつかまらないように、いつもまもっていた。デナリはこのくじらたちが大好きで、まるで自分のペットのように思っていた。

From time to time, Denali would see the whales as he was going about his summertime schedule. It was nice that the days were longer, for this gave him more time for whale-watching. Like Lani, he just knew somehow when and where the inseparable Putu, Siku and Kanik would surface. Sometimes at night, after saying his prayers, he couldn't get to sleep just imagining what it would be like to be a whale. Unfortunately, he couldn't explore or play in their frigid underwater world, like Lani could.

Most Eskimos eat a lot of whale meat, and Denali did, too. But of course, he would not let any whale hunters get near his three friends. They were like pets to him, and he loved them very much.

昼がすぎ、夜がすぎ、夏はあっというまにおわって、さむさがましてきた。デナリはちょっとしんぱいになってきて、プトゥとシクとカニクにテレパシーで話しかけた。ほかのくじらたちはほとんど、あたたかい南の海にたびだってしまったよ。きみたちもそうしたほうがいいよ。

ある日、やっとプトゥが、デナリの言うとおりだ、もう行かなくちゃ、とかんがえた。あたりまえだ！いつまでもこんな北のほうにのこっているのは、もう この３頭だけだった。あたりの海面があつい氷におおわれ、くうきをすうためのあなを見つけるのがむずかしくなっていた。

みんなが知っているように、くじらはほにゅうどうぶつで、くうきをすって生きている。長いじかん海にもぐっていられるが、ときどき海面に出て、くうきをすわなければ、しんでしまう。

プトゥとシクとカニクは、氷のあながたった一つしかのこっていなくて、そこからは、外の海にたどりつけないのにきがついた。たいへんなことになった。このあなだって、いまは大きくあいているけれど、すぐにほかのあなのように氷でふさがってしまうだろう。プトゥはあなのところに うかび上がって、デナリをよんだ。「たすけて！とじこめられちゃって、どうしたらいいかわからない！」

The summer days and nights slipped all too quickly away and the weather turned colder. Denali started to get a bit worried. He told Putu, Siku and Kanik with his mind that they'd better do as many of their friends had already done — head down south again to warmer waters.

One day, Putu finally decided that Denali was right, that it was time to leave. In fact, the three whales were the only ones left that far north... and it's no wonder! Thick ice had formed over most of the water and breathing holes were getting hard to find.

Everyone knows that whales are mammals and must breathe air to stay alive. They can stay beneath the water for long periods of time, but then they must come up for air, or they will die.

Soon Putu, Siku and Kanik realized that they couldn't find a way from their last ice hole to the open ocean. They were in big trouble. They did have one large air hole left, but it would soon be frozen over like all of the others. Putu rose to this spot and called for Denali, "Help us! We're trapped and don't know what to do!"

プトゥのさけびをきいて、くじらたちのところへ かけつけた デナリは、かれらのあわれなようすを見て、こころがしずんだ。カニクは、あの石あたまの あたらしいつかいみちにちょうせんしていた。氷のてんじょうにあたまや口さきをぶつけて、あなをあけようとしていたのだ。でも、ゆうかんなカニクのどりょくもむだで、カニクのあたまには、ほねが見えるほど深いきずがたくさんできて、ちだらけになっていた。プトゥとシクも、もうたのしいうたをうたうどころではなく、いきぐるしくてあえいでいた。3頭とも、とてもつかれて、とてもとてもこわがっていた。

　デナリは、何とかして友だちをたすけなくては、と思った。同じぶぞくのおとなのなかで「こどものころくじらと話せた」人たちに、くじらたちのことを大いそぎで知らせた。今までもくじらが氷の中にとじこめられたことがあって、それはみんな、おなかをすかせたほっきょくぐまに食べられてしまった。にんげんがたすけなければ、プトゥとシクとカニクもそうなってしまう！

enali heard Putu's cries and ran to find his friends. His heart was heavy when he saw how pitiful they looked. Kanik was now putting that hard head to new use. He was trying to use his head and beak to break through the ice and make new breathing holes. But all brave Kanik had to show for his efforts was a bloody scalp, cut to the bone in many places. Putu and Siku were no longer singing happy songs - they were gasping for air. All three whales were getting very tired, and were very, very scared.

　　Denali knew that he must try to help his friends. He rushed to tell some of the tribe's grown-ups who also "talked whale" about the sad situation. He knew that without human help, Putu, Siku and Kanik would end up like some other whales that had been trapped by the ice - as food for the hungry polar bears.

わいそうな３頭のくじらの話は、デナリの友だちから、またその友だちへとつたわって、やがて世界中に広まった。デナリとおなじように、このくじらたちをすくうためにできるだけのことをすべきだ、という人たちもいた。それでなくても、ザトウクジラは、ちきゅうからいなくなってしまう、としんぱいされているしゅぞくなのだ。いぜんは15,000頭のザトウクジラが、アラスカからハワイやカリフォルニアへとかいゆうしていたのに、今はたった2,500頭ぐらいしかのこっていない。むかし、にんげんは、あまりにもたくさんのくじらをとって、ころした。今はそのつぐないをするときだ。

ニュースをつたえる人々が、世界中からシクとプトゥとカニクのしゃしんをとりにきた。それで世界中の人々が、ぜったいぜつめいのききにおちいったかわいそうなくじらのしゃしんを見た。ラニも見た。ラニはこのくじらたちが、自分のたいせつな友だちだということは知らなかったけれど、毎晩テレビのニュースを見たあとで、かれらのためにいのった。世界の人々のどうじょうがプトゥとシクとカニクのもとによせられ、ちえのある人たちが、このくじらたちをたすけるほうほうをかんがえだそうとした。

デナリたち、エスキモーの人たちは、くじらたちのそばにいて、うたをうたったり、からだをなでたり、たった一つのこった氷のあながふさがらないようにしたりしてなぐさめた。それから、氷のない海へむかう道をつけようと、あたらしいあなをけずりはじめた。

Soon Denali's friends told their friends and it wasn't long before the whole world knew about these three whales whose future looked very dim. Some humans agreed with Denali that everything possible should be done to save them. After all, humpback whales are endangered species. While 15,000 of them used to make the round trip between Alaska and Hawaii or California, now only about 2,500 remain. In earlier times, man had hunted and killed too many whales. Now it was man's chance to make amends.

Newsmen came from all over the world to take pictures of Siku, Putu and Kanik. Soon people living all over the world, including Lani, saw pictures of the poor, desperate creatures. Every night after the TV news, Lani prayed for the whales, not knowing that these were her own dear friends. The heart of the whole world went out to Putu, Siku and Kanik, and the cleverest of minds tried to think of ways to save the whales.

Denali and other Eskimos kept the whales company and comforted them by singing to them, petting them and by keeping the one remaining breathing hole open. Then they started chipping new holes through the ice in a path toward the unfrozen waters.

いろいろな国のぎしたちが、どうすればくじらをにがすためのすいろがほれるかかんがえた。けれども、どんなすばらしい思いつきも、しぜんの大きな力の前では、まったくむだに見えた。氷はどんどんあつくなるばかりで、けっしてうすくはならない。きおんもぐんぐん下がっていく。やがて、この3頭のくじらをたすけるために、たくさんのおかねやじかんをかけるのはむだだ、という人も出てきた。

ある日、よわりきって、こきゅうをつづける力をうしなったカニクが、とうとう氷の下にしずんでしまった。プトゥとシクは、エスキモーの人たちが、くじらとりのりょうしもみんないっしょになって、あつさ15センチの氷をけずり、てんてんとあなをあけていくあいだ、なんとか持ちこたえていた。氷の海をふちどっているぶあつい氷のかべさえぬければ、そこは自由の海だ。

デナリはけっしてきぼうをうしなわなかった。世界中の人々が、このくじらたちのために、こころを一つにして、ちえを出しあっている。人々のあいと思いやりが、きっと友だちをこんなんからすくってくれるにちがいない。

デナリは正しかった。長いあいだ「冷戦」をつづけてきた国どうしが、くじらをすくうためにあゆみより、力をあわせようとしていた。ついに、これらの国々をへだててきた氷のかべがとけはじめたのだ。

Engineers from several countries tried to think of ways to break a channel through the ice to free the whales. But all of their great ideas seemed doomed, for Mother Nature just wouldn't cooperate. The ice grew thicker, not thinner. The temperature kept dropping. And some humans were beginning to say that it was not worth so much time and money to save three trapped whales.

One day Kanik disappeared under the ice forever, too exhausted to continue the struggle to breathe. Somehow Putu and Siku held on longer while Eskimos, some of them whalers, sawed a long line of new breathing holes through the six-inch ice toward a frozen ridge that was the last barrier to their freedom.

Denali never gave up hope. After all, the whole world was putting collective heads and hearts together, and somehow all of that love and concern would save his two struggling friends.

He was right. Countries that had long been fighting their own "cold war" were now coming together to cooperate to save the whales. At last the icy barrier that had long separated those countries had begun to thaw.

とうとう、2せきのさいひょうせんがやってきて、プトゥとシクの400メートル手前のところまで、氷のかべをきりひらいた。2頭のくじらは、100人をこす人々が見まもり、おうえんする中を、いのちがけでおよいだ。そして、ついに、とじこめられていたとうめいなおりからだっしゅつした！さいひょうせんの作ったすいろに、くじらたちがうかびあがるのを見て、デナリはかんせいをあげた！

その夜、デナリもラニも、自分と世界中の人々のねがいをかなえてくれたかみさまにかんしゃのおいのりをした。プトゥとシクは、生きるきかいをあたえられたのだ。そして、3頭のくじらもまた、じんるいに生きのこるきかいをあたえた。あいとへいわのために、ともに生き、ともに力をつくすことをおしえた。

Finally two icebreaker ships arrived and plowed through the last icy ridge to within 400 yards of Putu and Siku. As more than a hundred humans watched and cheered, the two whales swam for their lives from their crystal prison... and they made it! Denali shouted with joy as he saw them surface in the channel made by the ships!

That night Denali and Lani thanked God for answering their prayers and the prayers of the whole world. Putu and Siku had been given a second chance on life. And the three whales had given a second chance to all mankind — to learn to live and work together with peaceful purpose and love.

つぎの日、デナリは、くじらたちがまだすいろのところにいるのを見ておどろいた。デナリはエスキモーのことばで「ウウミク」、またね、と言いながら手をふり、プトゥとシクがゆっくり、しずかにおよぎさるのを見おくった。くじらたちがむきをかえ、さようならとありがとうのきもちをこめて、ひれをふった。らいねんの夏、またこの２頭に会えるんだ、とデナリにはわかっていた。

The next day Denali was surprised to see his friends still resting in the channel. He waved to them, saying "Uumiku," which is Eskimo for "next time," and he watched Putu and Siku slowly and silently swim away. They turned and, with their flippers, waved a special good-bye and thank you to their friend, and Denali knew that he would see them again next summer.

Biographies

スザーン・キタ　Suzanne Kita

高校教師、大学講師を経て現在、作家、編集者、教育コンサルタントとして活躍。詩作や新聞、雑誌記事の執筆に加え、アイランドヘリテージ社からは、ベストセラーとなった本作の英語版 (1996 年) と*Willie's Wallabies* (2000 年) を出版。家族とともにコロラド州のロッキーマウンテンに住み、絶滅寸前の生物や環境問題、それに、全人類の連携をテーマに子どもとおとなの両方を対象として本づくりをしている。

スティーブ・サンドラム　Steve Sundram

マウイ島在住のアーチスト。独学で学んだ。環境をテーマにした神秘的で不思議な雰囲気の画風で知られる。作品は、ポスター、アートカレンダー、CDジャケット、Tシャツ、パズル、絵本など様々の製品となり、世界中で出版されている。「私にとって芸術とは自分の愛するものを創造すること。この楽園の島々は、地球上で私が愛するものの全てを映し出している。」とサンドラムは言う。

オーシロ笑美　Emi I. Oshiro

カナダ、ブリティッシュコロンビア大学卒。東京で翻訳活動をしている。訳書には、世界各国で人気のあるコリン・マクノートン作『あっ、あぶない！』（ほるぷ出版、1997年）などがある。